Think all princesses are royal?

Think again!

Lorelei is sweet and pretty, but totally useless at housework. Prince Nicholas's parents meanwhile are holding a competition to find the Perfect Princess for their son. Will Lorelei pass all the tests and save Prince Nicholas from the horrible lip-licking crocodile princess?

SPINNING TALES

stories turned on their heads!

SPINNING TALES

the Princess Test

GAIL CARSON LEVINE

Collins

An imprint of HarperCollins*Publishers*

First published as *The Princess Tales: The Princess Test*
in the USA by HarperCollins Children's Books 1999
First published in Great Britain by Collins 2001

3 5 7 9 10 8 6 4

Collins is an imprint of HarperCollins*Publishers* Ltd,
77-85 Fulham Palace Road, Hammersmith, London W6 8JB

The HarperCollins website address is www.**fire**and**water**.com

ISBN 0 00 710946 6

Printed and bound in England by
Clays Ltd, St Ives plc

Once upon a time, in the village of Snettering-on-Snoakes in the Kingdom of Biddle, a blacksmith's wife named Gussie gave birth to a baby girl. Gussie and her husband, Sam, named the baby Lorelei, and they loved her dearly.

Lorelei's smile was sweet and her laughter was music. But as an infant she smiled only four times and laughed twice. The rest of the time she cried.

She cried when her porridge was too hot or too cold or too salty or too bitter or too sweet. She cried when her bathwater was too hot or too cold or too wet or not wet enough. She cried when her nappy was scratchy or smelly or not folded exactly right. She cried when her cradle was messy or when her mother forgot to make it with hospital corners. She cried whenever anything was not perfectly perfect.

Sam and Gussie did their best to make her happy. Lorelei was the only village baby with satin sheets and velvet nappies. She was the only one whose milk came from high-mountain yaks. And she was the only one who ate porridge made from two parts millet mixed with one part buckwheat. But still she cried.

She cried less as she learned to talk.

Then one day Lorelei said, "Father dearest and Mother dearest, I'm terribly sorry for crying so much. You have been too good to me."

Gussie said, "Oh honey, it's all right."

Sam said, "Gosh, we thought you were the cutest, best baby in this or any other kingdom."

Lorelei shook her head. "No. I was difficult. But I shall try to make it up to you. And now that I can explain myself, everything will be much better." She smiled. Then she sneezed. And sneezed again. She smiled shakily. "I fear I have a cold."

From then on, Lorelei stopped crying. She didn't stop being a picky eater, and she didn't stop needing everything to be just so. She just stopped crying about it.

Instead, Lorelei started being sick and having accidents.

If a child in the village of Snettering-on-Snoakes had a single spot, Lorelei caught the measles. If a child two villages and a mountain away had the mumps, Lorelei caught them, and the flu besides.

She loved the other children, and they liked her well enough. But if she played tag with them, she was sure to trip and skin her knee or her elbow or her chin. When they played hopscotch, she always twisted her ankle. Once, when she tried to jump rope, she got so tangled up that Gussie had to come and untie her.

When Lorelei turned fourteen, Gussie died. Sam and Lorelei were heartbroken. Sam swore never to marry again because Gussie was the sweetest wife anybody could ever have.

"Besides," he added, "all the old tales say that stepmothers are mean to their stepdaughters. You'll never have to worry about that, Lorelei honey."

Sam knew that Lorelei couldn't cook and clean for him and be her own nurse too. Besides, he'd be leaving soon for his annual trip to shoe the horses of the Earl of Pildenue, and someone would have to take care of Lorelei while he was gone. So he looked around for a housekeeper.

A wench named Trudy had helped the shoemaker's

family when their twins were born. The shoemaker said that Trudy was a hard worker, so Sam hired her. Trudy wondered why a blacksmith with a grown daughter needed a housekeeper, but she took the job.

As soon as Trudy walked in the door, Lorelei ran to her, stumbled, and fell into Trudy's arms.

"Dear Trudy, I'll do anything to help you. To the outer limits of my meagre ability."

Nobody had ever called Trudy "dear" before. So she thought this could be a pretty cushy spot, even if she understood only one word in ten that the lass said. But then again, if the girl wanted to help, why were the dirty dishes piled as high as a horse's rear end? Trudy shrugged and pumped water into the sink. "Here, lass. You can start on these."

"Oh, good!" Lorelei took the soap and started to scrub a plate.

Trudy looked around for a mop.

"Oh dear," Lorelei said.

"What's amiss?"

Lorelei raised her arms out of the soapy water. Trudy was horrified. The girl's arms and hands were covered with a bright red rash.

"Does this happen whenever you wash a dish?" Trudy asked.

"I don't know. I've never washed one before."

Never washed a dish! Her poor dead mother had let her get away with that? Had the woman mistaken her daughter for a princess?

"Mother kept the unguents and the bandages in the hutch," Lorelei said.

Trudy opened the hutch door. There were enough potions and herbs and simples to set up shop as a wisewoman.

"That one. There." Lorelei pointed to a big jar.

Trudy spread the salve over Lorelei's rash.

"It has to be wrapped in clean linen." Lorelei pointed again.

Trudy wrapped up Lorelei's arms — three times. The first time the bandages were too tight. The next time they were too loose. An hour passed before Lorelei said they were just right.

At last! Trudy thought. Her Majesty is satisfied.

"The dressing has to be changed every two hours," Lorelei said. "I'm sorry to be such a bother."

Trudy frowned. It wasn't exactly Her Highness's fault, but over an hour had gone by and the dishes were still dirty. The floor hadn't been mopped, and there was a mountain of laundry in the basket. She'd be working half the night to get it all done.

Trudy worked half the night that night and every night. For a month she took off bandages and put on bandages. When the rash was gone, Lorelei offered to help again.

Trudy hadn't been able to do any spinning because of all the bandaging. Surely, she thought,

Her Majesty can't come to grief spinning. "Can you help me with the spinning?"

Lorelei smiled happily. Gussie had never let her near the spinning wheel. She knew exactly what to do, though, because she'd watched her mother so often. She sat down at the wheel and got started.

Trudy nodded. There. She began to dust.

"Oh dear."

Trudy turned around. Lorelei had stabbed herself in the hand with the spindle and blood was pouring on to the cottage's wooden floor. Trudy ran for the bandages.

While Trudy bandaged her, Lorelei apologised at least a thousand times. After that, Trudy spent an hour scrubbing blood off the wooden floor and wondering what the bungling ninny was good for.

Not much, Trudy soon discovered. Lorelei could hang laundry on the line, and she could make a bed neatly. But the only thing she was really good at was embroidery. And Trudy had no need for embroidery. What she needed was to scream, long and loud.

Every day Trudy got madder and madder. While she washed Lorelei's satin sheets, her ladyship would be sitting at her ease, embroidering by the window. As Trudy kneaded Lorelei's special millet-buckwheat bread, the lazy thing would be lying in bed because her poor little throat hurt. Or her poor little left eyebrow. Or her poor little big toe.

Then came the joyous moment when Trudy thought of doing Lorelei in. Cooking Her Highness's goose. Rubbing her pampered self o-u-t. *Out!* Trudy started whistling.

Lorelei looked up from embroidering the outline of a potato on one of Sam's breeches. She smiled. "I'm so glad you're happy here, Trudy."

"Oh, I am, lass. Happier every minute."

It was lunchtime in the nearby court of the king and queen of Biddle. Hermione rang her little bell to let the Royal Servants know they could bring out the first course.

The Chief Royal Lunchtime Serving Maid carried a platter heaped with crab cakes into the royal dining room. King Humphrey helped himself to a tiny crab cake. Queen Hermione helped herself to a tiny crab cake. Prince Nicholas took a dozen or so crab cakes and started eating.

King Humphrey tasted his crab cake. Queen Hermione tasted her crab cake. They shook their heads. Queen Hermione rang her bell again. The Chief Royal Lunchtime Serving Maid stepped up to the royal table.

"I'm so sorry," Queen Hermione said. "These crab cakes taste a bit too fishy to me."

"We beg to differ or disagree," the king boomed. "They're not fishy enough."

"Crab isn't a fish," Prince Nicholas said, chewing happily. "My compliments to the chef."

"Please bring grapefruit instead," the queen said.

The Chief Royal Lunchtime Serving Maid removed the platter. On her way into the kitchen she passed a counter where the royal lunch was laid out. There were platters of crusty beef Wellington, creamed potatoes, and asparagus in mustard sauce, and there was a basket of poppyseed popovers. And two plates of grapefruit sections, poached eggs, and dry toast.

At a long table the Royal Servants waited for their lunch. The Chief Royal Lunchtime Serving Maid handed the platter of crab cakes to the Chief Royal Steward at the head of the table. He took four or five cakes and passed the plate to the Chief Royal Housekeeper on his right.

"There would be more for us if the prince didn't eat so much," the Chief Royal Undergardener complained.

"Hush," the Chief Royal Housekeeper said. "We're lucky to serve two such finicky rulers. My cousin Mabel doesn't fare half so well at the Earl of Pildenue's castle. The earl and his family adore their food, adore their clothes, adore their furniture. She never gets anything."

Back in Snettering-on-Snoakes, Lorelei ate her

lunch of grapefruit, poached eggs, and dry toast, and patted her mouth with an embroidered napkin. Then she went out to hang embroidered laundry on the embroidered clothesline.

While she worked, she thought about her mother and Trudy. Her mother had been so good to her. And Trudy was too. They both worked so hard. She hadn't helped her mother much, or Trudy, even though she always wanted to.

Trudy looked tired sometimes, although she never complained. Gussie must have been tired too. But no matter how tired she might have been, her mother had always had a kiss and a hug for Lorelei. And even if the hugs had made Lorelei a little black and blue, she would have given anything to have them back again.

She wiped away a tear with the embroidered toe of Sam's hose.

Prince Nicholas, riding by, saw the tear. He had

gone out after lunch to get some fresh air. As soon as he had turned into the lane, he'd seen Lorelei. She looked pretty in the distance. As he got closer, she was still pretty. Not a raving beauty, but definitely pretty. Light-brown hair. Ordinary colour, but thick and wavy. Nose a little too big. But her eyes were big too. Enormous. And she had roses in her cheeks. You didn't see roses in the cheeks of the noble and stuck-up ladies at court.

Then he saw she was crying! A corner of his heart that had never been touched before was touched. He leaped off his steed. "Maiden!" he cried. "You weep!"

Lorelei turned and knocked over the laundry basket. Embroidered petticoats and tunics and bodices danced across the small muddy yard.

Prince Nicholas vaulted over the low fence and helped Lorelei gather up the wash. He picked up one of Sam's shirts, embroidered with three-legged stools. The stitchery was masterful. But why three-legged stools?

He asked, "Maiden, why were you crying? Perhaps I can be of service."

Lorelei blushed. He wasn't that handsome, but there was something regal about him. Who was he? "I was missing my mother, kind sir."

"Your mother is…"

"She died." Lorelei smiled bravely and gathered up the last item of laundry, a petticoat embroidered with tiny tea kettles.

The poor maiden was an orphan, Nicholas thought. Or half of one if her father was alive. "You have my most sincere sympathy, maiden." He wanted to say more but couldn't think of anything else.

Lorelei smiled. "Thank you, kind sir." He was nice!

She had a wonderful smile. He found himself

stammering. "Er… I am P-Prince N-Nicholas."

He was a prince! She swept him a curtsy. "I am Lorelei."

Inside, Trudy glanced up from her washtub. Look at Her Highness out there, she thought, passing the time with a young lord. Not for long, your ladyship. She hummed and danced a little jig. Not for long, hey-ho! Not for long, tra-la!

When Nicholas got back to the castle, King Humphrey summoned him to the throne room. As usual it was full of courtiers and subjects. King Humphrey had just settled an argument between two farmers over a cow. When he saw Nicholas, the king ordered everyone to leave. The only ones left were the king, the queen, the prince, and the Chief Royal Window Washer, who was cleaning the stained-glass windows.

"Son," King Humphrey boomed. "We are growing old or advancing in years. We should like to abdicate. But before we do, you must wed or get married."

Nicholas thought of Lorelei and his heart started to race. "I just met——"

"We must find you a true princess," Queen Hermione interrupted. "The descendant of a long line of royalty. A noble maiden, with..."

That eliminates Lorelei, Nicholas thought. Her pretty, rosy cheeks alone would rule her out.

"We've devised a test," the king said. "Or an examination."

"But what if I don't love the true princess?"

"You'll love her," Queen Hermione said. "She'll be just right for you."

No she won't! thought Nicholas.

"You'll make yourself love or adore her," King Humphrey roared. "Or we'll abdicate in favour of Archduke Percival."

Nicholas hated the archduke. Percy threw his servants into the moat if they did something wrong or if he felt like it. He would be a terrible king.

"Would you like to hear the test, dear?" the queen asked.

Nicholas nodded.

"When a maiden arrives who claims to be a true princess," Queen Hermione said, "we shall give her a bouquet."

The king guffawed. "But amidst all the fragrant or sweet-smelling flowers, there will be a sprig or small bunch of parsley. And that's not a flower."

Nicholas wondered what parsley had to do with being a princess.

"The true princess will know," the queen said. "She will pluck that parsley right out of her bouquet."

"That's the test?"

"Certainly not," Queen Hermione said. "There's more. We shall serve her a salad. A beautiful salad."

"Except," King Humphrey said, chuckling, "right in the middle, there will be a bit—"

"A speck—" the queen interrupted.

"The merest fleck. We don't want to hurt or injure the maiden. There will be a fleck of uncooked or raw noodle."

"The true princess will find it!" Queen Hermione announced.

What did parsley and noodles have to do with being a kind and just ruler? Nicholas listened in amazement to the rest of the test. There would be a trial in every course of the banquet. Also, the poor princess would be given a gown with a skirt that was a tint lighter than the bodice. She'd have to notice. She'd be shown a tapestry and would have to find the single missing stitch.

Lorelei might pass that one, Nicholas thought.

Every inch of the princess would be measured. Her waist had to be tiny. Her hands and feet had to be small, although her fingers had to be long. Her big toe had to be longer than her index toe. She had to be tall, but not a giant. And so on.

"But the final test will be the most important one," Queen Hermione said.

"There's more?" Nicholas said.

King Humphrey nodded solemnly. Then he nodded again.

"She will sleep in a guest bedroom," the queen said. "Her bed will be piled with twenty soft mattresses."

"She'll fall off!" Nicholas said. "She'll hurt—"

"A princess does not fall," the queen said. She went on. "Each mattress will be filled with the finest swans' feathers. But under the bottom mattress we will place a pea. If she sleeps well, she is no true princess!"

King Humphrey agreed. "If she sleeps or slumbers well, she is no true princess!"

The Chief Royal Chambermaid heard about the pea test from the Chief Royal Window Washer. It made her curious, so she got a pea from the Chief Royal Cook. A dried pea, because they couldn't have meant a fresh one, which would just squoosh flat.

The Chief Royal Chambermaid made everything ready, just as it would be for the princess. One pea. Twenty mattresses. And a ladder.

She climbed up. The bed was sooo soft. It was delicious. Pea? She couldn't feel any pea. With twenty mattresses under her, she doubted she would feel a watermelon. She didn't think anybody could feel the pea — true princess, fake princess, or any other kind.

The Chief Royal Chambermaid climbed down

and yanked off a few mattresses. Then she climbed back up. She still couldn't feel the pea. She pulled off more mattresses and tried again. Nothing.

She took off all the mattresses except the bottom one, but she still couldn't feel anything. She checked under the mattress. There it was. Well, she was no princess. Maybe a true princess could feel a pea under one or two mattresses. But under twenty? Not on your life.

5

Sam got ready for his trip to the earldom of Pildenue. The earl was his only noble customer. Sam made enough from this one job to keep Lorelei in silk kirtles and embroidery thread for a year.

He said a long farewell to Lorelei in front of their cottage. "Be sure you wear your shawl at night, honey."

"I will, Father."

"Be sure she does, Trudy. I don't want her to get sick."

"Yes, Master," Trudy said. Would that be a good way to bump her off? Let her catch cold and die?

"And make her eat enough, Trudy. You have to keep your strength up, sweetie pie."

"Yes, Master," Trudy said. Should she starve Lorelei? No. It would take too long.

"Here, sweet. Give your old daddy a kiss."

Lorelei hugged him. "I'll miss you, Father. Hurry home."

Sam climbed up to the seat of his wagon. He flapped the reins, and the old mare started to trot.

Lorelei wiped away a tear. She turned to Trudy. "We'll just have to keep each other company." She sniffled. "We'll have a lovely time, won't we?"

"Yes, lass." Yes indeed!

King Humphrey wrote a proclamation to announce the search for a real princess.

"Hear ye! Hear ye! Or listen well! Insofar and Inasmuch as We, King Humphrey, Supreme Ruler and Monarch of the Kingdom and Monarchy of Biddle…"

The king paused here. But there was no synonym for Biddle, so he went on.

"… Wish to Abdicate Our Throne in Favour of Our Son and Heir, the Noble and Royal Prince Nicholas. And Insofar and Inasmuch as We Stipulate and Require…"

And so on. The next important part came at the very end. "… and Said Princess Must Satisfy Us, King Humphrey, Supreme…" Blah blah blah. "… That She Is in Her Person and Her Self a Completely and Utterly True Princess. Our Judgement on This Matter or in This Respect Shall be Final and Without Appeal."

Below that King Humphrey signed *King Humphrey or Supreme Ruler of Biddle,* as was his habit. The Royal Seal was affixed, and the proclamation was complete. And finished, too.

Except for one thing. The king wanted a portrait of Prince Nicholas to go with the proclamation. He sent for his Chief Royal Artist and Portrait Maker.

"My son or heir isn't a bad-looking boy, is he?" King Humphrey asked the artist. "There's nothing wrong with his looks, is there?"

"Oh no, Sire. Not in the slightest." The Chief Royal Artist and Portrait Maker thought the prince was ordinary-looking. Nothing special.

"The prince has to look handsome in his portrait or picture," the king said. "That way a true princess will want and desire to come."

"I understand, sire." Smaller ears. Straighter mouth. Broader shoulders. He could do that.

Nicholas wanted to look as ugly as possible in his

portrait. He wanted every princess who saw it to say, "Ugh. Who would want to marry *him*?" Because if no princesses showed up, he might be able to convince the king and queen to let him marry Lorelei.

So he squinted. He squirmed. He mussed his hair. He let his mouth hang open. He drooled. He borrowed Queen Hermione's make-up and drew a big black mole on his chin.

It made no difference. The Chief Royal Artist and Portrait Maker was a master craftsman. In the portrait Prince Nicholas' chin (without a mole) was lifted majestically. His eyes had a piercing look. A hint of a smile played around his mouth. His shoulders were broad. His mouth wasn't lopsided. His ears were perfect. Also, the Chief Royal Artist and Portrait Maker waved Nicholas' hair and thickened his eyelashes. Princesses would fall in love with those eyelashes. Guaranteed.

When all was ready, scribes copied the proclamation. Lesser Royal Artists and Portrait Makers copied the portrait. Messengers were dispatched to kingdoms near and far.

The search was on.

6

Trudy thought about how to do Lorelei in. She could hit her over the head with the frying pan. Or strangle her with the embroidered clothesline. Or drag her to the village square and push her out of the clock tower. Any one of those would be lots of fun. But she'd be caught. The dopey villagers liked Lorelei.

It should be easy to finish her off, Trudy reasoned. After all, Her Highness was in bed sick or hurt three times a week without anybody doing anything to her. Why, she could murder herself one of these days without Trudy's having to lift a finger! Hmm. Now that was an idea.

The morning after Sam left, Trudy announced that she didn't feel well. "You'll have to do the housework today, lass," Trudy said. "I'm not up to it."

Lorelei would wash the dishes and she'd get that rash again. But today Trudy would be too sick to put on the salve. So Lorelei would swell up like a balloon and *POP*! And nobody would think it was Trudy's fault.

"Oh dear. Does your stomach ache?"

Trudy nodded.

"Oh dear. Does your forehead pulse?"

Trudy nodded.

"Your throat. Is it hard to swallow?"

Trudy nodded.

Lorelei clapped her hands. "Then I know just what to do. You've been so good to me, dear Trudy. And now I can help you." She threw open the door to the hutch and pulled out strangely shaped bottles and odd bundles of herbs.

"I used to get what you have," Lorelei said. "Mother made me well in a jiffy." She dumped whatever was in the bottles and bundles into a pot. Then she hung the pot on a hook in the fireplace.

Soon a sharp odour filled the room. Trudy's eyes watered. The hairs in her nose felt like they were burning.

"Doesn't it smell wonderful?" Lorelei asked. "I always feel better when I smell the steam. In a few minutes you'll drink the broth and be well again, dear Trudy."

She was going to have to *drink* that slop? Trudy

jumped up. "I feel much better. Fine. Really." She poured the disgusting brew on the fire. Stinky smoke billowed out. "You're a good wisewoman. You've cured me already." Trudy opened the cottage door and the windows. She could have been killed!

She started on the chores. What else could she do? Hmm. "Lass?"

"Yes, Trudy?"

"I'm off to the market. While I'm gone, would you like to try the spinning wheel again?"

"Oh yes!"

"I won't be long. Be careful with the spindle." Trudy shut the door behind her and sauntered down the lane. Her ladyship would stab herself again. By the time Trudy got back, Lorelei would have bled to death.

The market was busy. Trudy gossiped with the other shoppers. She told the pedlars what was wrong with their goods. She even bought herself a pink hair ribbon. Then she strolled back to the blacksmith's cottage. What a delightful day it was!

She opened the door. No, it was a terrible day! Lorelei wasn't bleeding. Not even a drop. The only thing that was hurt was the spinning wheel. It looked like a giant spider had spun a web all over it. It would take days to untangle the mess.

Lorelei was crying. "Oh, Trudy! I'm sorry. I wanted to have yards and yards of beautiful linen finished when you got back. You must be so disappointed in me."

Lorelei couldn't understand what Trudy was saying. It sounded something like "Argul! Gloog! Blub!" Trudy yanked open the cottage door and slammed it behind her. She stood on the doorstep, panting. She had to get a grip on herself. She couldn't let that little… that little good-for-nothing fancy *idiot* do this to her.

She had to plan it out better. She had plenty of time. Two months before Sam came home. Plenty of time.

Lorelei was as good as dead.

A month went by and no one arrived at the court of Biddle to take the princess test. Queen Hermione smiled knowingly. She said the young ladies were getting ready, having gowns made, making themselves beautiful for their prince.

Making themselves as princessy as possible, Nicholas thought. I want Lorelei! He wanted to cry.

Every day he rode to her lane in the village of Snettering-on-Snoakes. He spent hours watching the smoke curl out of her chimney. He didn't even have to see her. Just seeing the smoke was enough.

But sometimes he did see her, sitting at her window, embroidering. He'd wonder what she was sewing. Buckets? Doorknobs? Galoshes? He thought his heart would break in two pieces.

One day Lorelei was outside, picking roses from the bush outside the cottage door. She turned when she heard the clatter of his horse's hooves. It was that nice prince again, she thought. What was his name? Nicholas. A nice name. She curtsied.

Nicholas jumped off his horse. He bowed. What could he say to her? "Er… hello, maid Lorelei."

She smiled. "Hello, Your Highness."

"Fine weather we're having." He wished he could think of something more interesting to say.

"I think the clouds could mean rain." Why

couldn't she think of something more interesting to say? He probably knew a hundred princesses who could make fascinating conversation.

"Those roses are pretty. Did you plant them?"

Inside the cottage Trudy was cleaning the stove. She saw Lorelei through the window and wished the sluggard would prick herself with a poisoned thorn. She wished that the young lord talking to Lorelei were a highwayman who would kidnap her. Then he'd have to clean up after her and bandage her. Then she'd be his problem.

Hmm... Trudy thought, that's it! That's the way to get rid of her, once and for all.

The very next day a princess showed up at King Humphrey's court. She was Princess Cordelia from the nearby kingdom of Kulornia.

King Humphrey himself helped her down from her carriage.

She was good-looking. The king didn't have his tape measure with him, but she seemed tall enough. And her hands looked the right size.

Queen Hermione smiled. The maiden looked promising.

Prince Nicholas frowned and bowed. He could tell already. He didn't like Cordelia.

"Thank you." She curtsied. "Well, well, well. Here I am. We made good time getting here. We only stopped three times on the road. Traffic wasn't bad. Dandy courtyard you have here, Humphrey. Hello, Nicky. I see they exaggerated on your portrait. I expected that, so don't worry about it. They always do it in the marriage game. Well, well. Dandy courtyard…"

Queen Hermione looked at her husband. They had forgotten to put in a test for the art of conversation.

King Humphrey looked at his wife. They had

forgotten to put in a test for talking your head off or never shutting up.

Nicholas looked at the sky. Nicky! He mustn't scream. He didn't have to marry anybody yet.

The king snapped his fingers. The Chief Royal Bouquet Maker stepped forward. He presented a bouquet to Princess Cordelia.

Let her not find the parsley. Nicholas prayed.

Let her not find the parsley or herb, the king prayed.

Let her not find the parsley, the queen prayed.

"Well, well, well. You folks sure know how to roll out the red carpet. There's nothing like a bunch of flowers to brighten things up. Take a dull tower room and—"

"Would you like us to put them in water, my dear?" Queen Hermione asked. If she said yes, it would be all over.

"Sure. Wouldn't want them to go limp and

croak right in—"

"We're so glad you had a comfortable journey," King Humphrey interrupted firmly. "We hope or desire that it will be even better going the other way. Thank you so much for coming." He handed her back into the carriage and slapped the horses to get them moving quickly or rapidly.

Princess Cordelia stuck her head out of the window. "Well! What did I do? I thought we were getting along just fine. When you issue a..."

The three of them went back into the castle. They could hear Cordelia yelling till the heavy doors thudded shut behind them.

8

On the same day that the talkative Princess Cordelia was thrown out of Biddle, Trudy perfected her plan. She would lose Lorelei, plain and simple. And whoever found her would have to keep her — finders keepers. Trudy giggled.

"Lass," Trudy said. "What's the name of that herb you like in your tea sometimes?"

"Hyssop?"

"That's the one. We're fresh out of it, and there's none in the market."

"That's all right." Lorelei smiled bravely. "I can do without."

"But I don't want you to, sweet. I want you to be happy, honey lamb."

"You're so good to me."

Hah! "Tim, the spice pedlar, told me where it grows in the forest. I thought we could harness your dad's mule and go there tomorrow. We'll have a picnic."

"What fun!"

Hooray! Trudy thought. The bumbling ninny would never find her way home from the middle of the forest.

The next day princesses arrived at the castle in droves. They came in carriages drawn by horses, by camels, by oxen. One even came in a carriage drawn by crocodiles. And another arrived in a hot-air balloon. The courtyard was clogged with animals and carriages and princesses. The Royal Guards got tired of raising and lowering the drawbridge. They decided to leave it lowered till the prince announced his engagement.

There were too many princesses to test one by one. So the king and queen decided to test them all together.

Nicholas looked them over. Some were too short. Some were too tall. Some were too thin. Some were too fat. They'd all fail the measurement test. But the rest seemed about right. The most beautiful princess was the one who'd come in the carriage pulled by crocodiles. She had huge purple eyes and a slow smile. She gave Nicholas the shivers. He kept feeling she didn't want to marry him — she really wanted to roast him and eat him with cream sauce.

∞

In the forest Lorelei finished weaving a daisy chain. She was in a small clearing, sitting on an embroidered blanket, a velvet embroidered blanket, of course. The only kind that didn't make her itchy.

Trudy was hunting for hyssop, the herb for Lorelei's tea.

"Do you see any?" Lorelei called.

"Not yet. Eat your lunch. I'll be there soon."

Lorelei opened the picnic basket. Trudy's voice sounded far away. Lorelei bit into her cucumber sandwich with the crusts cut off. "Trudy!" she called. "Come back. You must be hungry."

"Soon. I think I see something."

Lorelei could hardly hear the words. It was too bad that Trudy couldn't enjoy this beautiful day. The spice pedlar should have drawn a map showing exactly where the hyssop grew. Lorelei finished her lunch and leaned back on the blanket. Such sweet puffy white clouds. She closed her eyes. In a few minutes she was asleep.

Trudy led Leonard the mule along the trail next to the stream. Lorelei hadn't called in a while. It was safe to stop. Trudy tied Leonard to a tree and took the extra lunch out of his saddlebag. She kicked off her shoes and sat on a rock with her feet dangling in the cool water. She bit into her sandwich. Sausages and peppers. Her favourite. This was peace.

Prince Nicholas couldn't stand being around all these princesses for another minute. He saddled his horse and rose to Snettering-on-Snoakes. He had to see Lorelei.

But she wasn't there. Her cottage was empty.

The first drops of rain woke Lorelei. The sky was dark.

"Trudy?"

A roll of thunder drowned her out. The drops came down harder. They were huge.

"Trudy? Do you hear me?"

Had Trudy come back and eaten her lunch while she was asleep? Lorelei opened the basket. No. Trudy's sausage-and-peppers sandwich was still there. Trudy is lost! Lorelei thought. Poor Trudy. She must be terrified.

Lightning lit the sky. Were you supposed to get under a tree when there was lightning? Or stay away from trees?

At least she'd be drier under a tree. Lorelei jumped up and folded the blanket neatly. Then she took the picnic basket and ran under a tall maple.

She stayed under the tree for an hour. Every few minutes she called Trudy, but there was never an answer. The sky grew darker. Storm dark, but also night dark. Lorelei's stomach rumbled delicately. Time for dinner.

She had to find Trudy. It was her responsibility because she was Trudy's mistress. She had never felt so full of purpose before. She had to find Trudy and Leonard the mule and get them home safely. She'd go to the stream first. The last time she'd heard Trudy's voice, it had come from there.

The stream was across the clearing and straight ahead, through a stand of trees. Lorelei stepped into the clearing and was drenched instantly. Oh well, she thought. It was only water.

"Trudy! Stay where you are. I'm coming." She didn't want poor Trudy to have one second more of terror than she had to.

As the water soaked into them, Lorelei's skirts got heavier and heavier and dragged more and more. It was hard to walk, but she had to do it.

"Trudy! I'm coming!"

Where was the stream? She should have reached it by now.

"Leonard?" Maybe the mule would hee-haw and she'd find him. Then she could ride him and find Trudy more quickly. She pushed past bushes and over fallen logs.

Two hours passed. Lorelei still hadn't found Leonard, Trudy, or the stream. She was hungry and chilled. She sneezed almost as often as she took a breath. She couldn't get sick, not now when Trudy needed her.

Finally Lorelei sat on a tree stump and cried between sneezes. She had to admit it. Trudy was lost. Leonard was lost. And she was lost.

By dinnertime the flood of princesses had slowed to a trickle. Around ten o'clock it stopped. Seventy-nine princesses had come.

Queen Hermione set aside a wing of the castle just for them. Tonight they would sleep in ordinary beds with only one mattress and no pea. Tomorrow the tests would begin. Tomorrow night would be the final exam for those who had passed all the other tests. The mattress and pea test. The test that the Chief Royal Chambermaid was sure nobody could pass.

Prince Nicholas was beside himself. What was he going to do? And where was Lorelei?

Lorelei was flat on her face in the forest. She had tripped over a tree root, and she was too tired to get up. Too tired to do anything except sneeze.

But she had to get back to the village and form a search party. She stood and picked up the picnic basket and blanket. Her gown and face were covered with mud and dead leaves. Well, the rain would clean off her face. And the gown didn't matter, since she hadn't had a chance to embroider anything on it yet.

She heard something. She stood still and fought back a sneeze. There it was again. A snuffling noise.

Trudy! She opened her mouth to yell. But wait. What if it wasn't Trudy. What if it was—

Lorelei had never climbed a tree in her life. But she climbed one now. One second she was on the ground. The next she was twelve feet up.

A bear crashed through the bushes. She sneezed. Oh no! He was going to find her!

But he passed right by, in a big hurry. He didn't even look up. He was probably going to his nice warm cave. Lucky bear.

Lorelei climbed down from the tree and stumbled on. "Achoo!" Hang on, Trudy, she thought. Hang on, I'm coming.

Nicholas couldn't sleep. He paced up and down in his room. He didn't want to marry anyone but Lorelei. He didn't care about having a princess for a bride. As soon as he married her, Lorelei would be a princess anyway. So what was the difference?

He wouldn't even care that much about becoming a king someday, if Archduke Percy wasn't such a monster.

The wind howled in the forest beyond the moat. He looked out of his window. Sheets of rain poured down. Wherever Lorelei had been today, she'd have to be home by now. He wished he could peek in her window and see her, warm and dry and fast asleep, in an embroidered nightgown.

Had she seen a light? Way up ahead? So much water was coming down, it was hard to keep her eyes open. "Achoo!"

Lightning flashed, and Lorelei saw a castle. Towers and battlements, dark against the yellow-grey sky.

Who lived there? A royal family? A troll family? Ogres? An evil magician? Maybe she should stay in the forest. "Achoo!" No. She had to go on. For Trudy's sake.

She hurried across the drawbridge. "Achoo!" It would be dry inside. She'd be out of the wind. If the owner was an ogre and he decided to eat her, she'd warm up while she roasted. And if he was a decent ogre, he might even let her take a bath before he cooked her.

She knocked on the thick oak doors. The Chief Royal Night Watchman opened them. A dripping muddy maiden stood there. Another princess? She didn't look like much. But he had his orders, and he let her into the great hall. "Wait here," he barked.

Nicholas had seen the small figure cross the drawbridge. Another one, he thought. His parents weren't going to like having to get up in the middle of the night for her. He grinned sourly. They'd be sorry they hadn't put in a test for coming in the daytime.

He met his parents on the circular stairway to the

great hall where the maiden stood shivering and sneezing.

He couldn't believe it. It was Lorelei! What was she doing here?

Lorelei watched them come down the stairs. They weren't ogres and trolls. One of them even looked familiar. It was that nice Prince Nicholas. Lorelei's heart lurched a little.

She curtsied deeply. She sneezed and wobbled and almost fell over.

They have kind faces, Lorelei thought, but they looked annoyed. Except the prince. He looks glad to see me. She sent him a special smile. And then she sneezed.

"Who are you?" King Humphrey boomed. "Which one are you?"

"I am – achoo! – Lorelei. You see – achoo! – I got—"

"Another princess," Nicholas interrupted loudly.

"There's always room for one more." He winked at Lorelei, hoping she'd see and go along. Hoping his parents wouldn't see. "Who knows?" he added. "She might be the one to pass the princess tests."

Lorelei saw the wink. He wanted her to pretend to be a princess? She could, if he wanted her to. But why?

She curtsied again. "I am Princess Lorelei. Achoo!"

"How did you get here?" Queen Hermione asked. "Where's your carriage?"

"Um… achoo! Um. I don't have a carriage. Um…" What could she say? "Um… I… I was bewitched." That was it! "Achoo! A fairy put a spell on our whole court. My father was turned into a blacksmith. I became a blacksmith's daughter. I was

— achoo! — a baby when it happened."

Quick thinking, Nicholas thought. She was clever, too.

"Absurd! Ridiculous!" King Humphrey roared. "There hasn't been a case or example of a fairy spell in a hundred years. Not since Queen Rosella and King Harold's reign."

"Achoo!"

The lass is crazy, the queen thought.

"Suppose she is a true princess?" Prince Nicholas said. "She might be the only one of the eighty maidens here who is." He hoped Lorelei was paying attention. "If you don't give her the tests, you'll never know. You won't be able to abdicate, Father. I'll never marry. You'll never have grand—"

"Son or heir, you're right." The king put an arm around Nicholas' shoulder. "The boy is correct or accurate."

Lorelei listened between sneezes. Tests? Had they

said that if she passed some tests, she could marry Nicholas? Really?

Queen Hermione shrugged. It couldn't do any harm. A true blacksmith's daughter would certainly fail the tests. She rang her bell for the Chief Royal Chambermaid.

"Achoo! Excuse me. My Lady-in-Waiting was with me when we got lost. Achoo! She's still under the spell. She thinks she keeps house for a blacksmith." Lorelei told them about Trudy.

She's so kind! Nicholas thought.

"And our black stallion got lost too. He looks like a mule."

The king called for a groom to ride to the village of Snettering-on-Snoakes to see if Trudy and Leonard had got home safely.

Lorelei went upstairs with the Chief Royal Chambermaid. Nicholas followed them. She'll pass one test anyway, he thought, looking at her muddy footprints. She has small feet. But what about the rest?

The tests began first thing in the morning.

Lorelei had slept well. Her sheets were satin. The blankets were velvet. The mattress was stuffed with swans' feathers. Just like home. When she woke up, she wasn't even sneezing any more.

Someone had laid a gown out for her, and a Royal Chambermaid was there to dress her. The gown was pretty, with diamonds sewn into the skirt and pearls sewn into the bodice. But it wasn't embroidered, which was a shame. And look at that! "That's funny," she said out loud.

The Royal Chambermaid curtsied. "What's funny, your ladyship?"

"Well..." You'd think they'd get it right for a princess. "The skirt on the gown – I don't mean to criticise – but it's lighter than the bodice."

So Lorelei passed the first test.

Three princesses hadn't noticed. Seventy-seven maidens sat down to breakfast, which was a simple meal. Poached eggs, dry toast, and half a grapefruit — Lorelei's favourite food for breakfast, lunch, and dinner.

While they ate, King Humphrey welcomed them to the kingdom or monarchy of Biddle. Then he explained about the tests, but he didn't say what any of them were. "In closing," he concluded, "let the truest princess conquer or win."

After breakfast, the king and queen and Nicholas gave the princesses and Lorelei a tour of the castle. King Humphrey lectured about Biddle as they went. Nicholas stayed near Lorelei, wishing he could warn her about each test, but the princesses might hear.

When the tour was over, everyone returned to the royal banquet hall for lunch — the next round in the true-princess test (although the contestants didn't know it).

The queen rang her bell, and Royal Serving Maids entered the royal banquet hall.

A salad was placed in front of Lorelei. She picked up her fork.

Now why was a bit of uncooked noodle mixed in with the lettuce? Quietly, she pointed it out to the Royal Serving Maid. And passed the salad test. So that was it, Lorelei thought. You had to guess what was wrong with the food. Funny test.

Five maidens didn't find the noodle. They were escorted out immediately.

Seventy-one to go, Nicholas thought. He noticed that the crocodile princess was still in the running.

Lorelei found the toothpick under the flounder. It wasn't hard, now that she knew what to look for. Nicholas breathed a sigh of relief.

Only one princess didn't find the toothpick.

Lorelei fished the tiny marshmallow out of her ragout. Eight princesses didn't. One of them was dragged away, yelling, "It isn't fair! Mine melted!"

Nicholas thought he was going to die of worry before the meal ended.

Lorelei found the flake of tuna on the chocolate cake icing. Four princesses didn't. The meal was over. Lorelei and the crocodile princess and fifty-seven other princesses remained in the game.

After lunch the measuring began in the queen's bedchamber.

Nicholas and the king weren't allowed to view this part of the test. They waited in the throne room. King Humphrey listened to petitions from his subjects while Nicholas paced up and down chewing his nails.

In the bedchamber Royal Chambermaids with

tape measures checked every inch of every princess. If a princess was too tall, she was out. If she was too short, she was out. If her ears were too big, they were out and she was out.

The measuring took the rest of the day. Lorelei worried about the size of her nose. It was her worst feature. She pulled in her nostrils. When she looked in the mirror, she always thought that made her nose seem a little smaller.

Her nose squeaked by. A hair bigger and she would have had it.

The measuring went on.

The waist of one of the princesses was too big by a sixty-fourth of an inch. Queen Hermione said she was sorry, but if she let this maiden slip by, she wouldn't know where to draw the line.

When the measuring was over, only ten princesses and Lorelei were left. The queen led them to the throne room.

The crocodile princess entered first. Nicholas bit his finger so hard it bled. She smiled at him. Her teeth looked pointy. Where was Lorelei? He held his breath.

Lorelei was the ninth to enter the room. Nicholas started breathing again. They looked at each other. This was scary.

The king gave bouquets to the princesses and congratulated or applauded them on getting so far.

Nicholas wanted to yell, It's another trick! It's a test!

Lorelei held her bouquet away from her to examine it. Some flowers made her sneeze and some made her eyes water. Roses were OK. Daffodils were OK too. Lilies made her sneeze. So did peonies. What was that? Parsley? That wasn't a flower. This was a test! She pulled out the parsley and sneezed.

The bouquet test fooled everyone except the crocodile princess and Lorelei. The best and the worst, Prince Nicholas thought. He was trembling.

Both of them passed the tapestry test. Lorelei spotted the missing thread from twenty feet away. Nicholas wished she could get extra credit.

King Humphrey announced that they would have a light supper and go to bed. The final test or examination, he lied, would be tomorrow, or the day after today.

Lorelei didn't have a moment to talk privately with Nicholas. She could tell he wanted her to be the one to pass the test, but she wanted to hear him say it. She also wanted him to give her a hint about the big test tomorrow.

He wanted to get near her, too. If he could whisper to her for just one second, he could tell her about the pea. But at supper she sat at the other end of the table, next to the king. Nicholas heard him telling her about his collection of unicorn horns or tusks.

The crocodile princess sat between the king and queen. Nicholas hated the way she ate. She seemed to swallow her food without chewing. And she kept looking at him and licking her lips.

Nicholas excused himself from the table. He went out to the garden and picked up a few large rocks. Then he slipped back into the castle and headed for Lorelei's bedchamber. He'd put the rocks under the top mattress, where she'd be sure to feel them.

But he couldn't get in. The Chief Royal Guard stood in front of the door. Nicholas tried to send him on an errand, but the fellow said that the king had told him not to budge for anyone or any person.

So then Nicholas said he'd leave a note for Princess Lorelei. But the Chief Royal Guard said, "Begging your pardon, Your Highness, no notes. I have my orders."

Nicholas couldn't do anything. By this time

tomorrow either he'd be engaged to Lorelei, or Percival would be the future King of Biddle. Or he'd be engaged to the crocodile princess!

12

Nicholas couldn't sleep. One second he was full of hope. She'd passed all the tests so far! The next second he was in despair. Nobody could feel a pea through all those mattresses. And the crocodile princess had a better chance than Lorelei. After all, the crocodile princess was a real princess, not a blacksmith's daughter.

But it didn't matter. If Lorelei failed, he'd marry her anyway. And his parents would have fits. And Percival would get the throne. He tossed. He turned. He finally slept, and he dreamed of being eaten by crocodiles and drowned in peas.

When Lorelei entered her room, she wondered why her bed had so many mattresses. Last night it had been an ordinary bed. She shrugged. Maybe they wanted her to have an extra-good night's sleep before the big test.

She climbed the ladder and slipped under the sheets. The bed was the softest she'd ever been in. She stretched and wriggled her toes. Mmm. Lovely!

The prince was so nice! Even if he weren't a prince, even if he were a blacksmith, she'd love him. But he *was* a prince, and that was even better.

She rolled over. She couldn't get comfortable. The sheets felt all right. Satin. Satin was good. The blankets were velvet. Velvet was good.

She closed her eyes.

Something was wrong. Her nose itched and her back ached. She climbed down from the bed and looked at it.

It had to be the mattresses. Maybe there was a pigeon feather in one of them. But which one? There were so many.

She'd never fall asleep. She'd be up all night. Then she wouldn't be at her best for the big test tomorrow. Maybe she could stretch out in front of the fireplace.

She spread a blanket on the floor and laid another one on top of it. Then she got in between them and closed her eyes. The hours crawled by. The floor was hard, but you expected a floor to be uncomfortable. You didn't expect it from a bed piled with twenty mattresses.

Lorelei turned over on her stomach. No better.

She rolled back. Could she, Lorelei, actually become a princess? She'd passed every test so far. If she married Prince Nicholas, she'd live in a castle. And so would her father. She giggled. Trudy would be a real lady-in-waiting.

Trudy! She sat up. She'd forgotten to find out if Trudy had got home safely. What kind of queen would she make if she couldn't remember her subjects?

She lay down again. She'd ask first thing in the morning. What could the test tomorrow be like? Would they ask her questions? She didn't know anything about being a princess. She didn't know much about being a blacksmith's daughter either.

What if they asked her about laws! About geography! About how to sit on a throne! Lorelei was awake all night.

In the morning the Chief Royal Chambermaid led

the two maidens to the throne room. Lorelei's bones ached, and the skin under her gown was black and blue.

King Humphrey and Queen Hermione and Prince Nicholas were sitting on their thrones. All the courtiers and subjects had been cleared out for the big moment.

The first thing Lorelei wanted to do was to find out about Trudy. Then she'd take whatever test they wanted. She'd probably fail it. But at least she'd know about Trudy.

The other maiden looked so rested and… Lorelei hated to admit it, but the other one was beautiful. Maybe by now Nicholas wanted her to win.

"Good morning, princesses or damsels," the king boomed.

"Did you sleep—" the queen began.

"Did you find out—" Lorelei began.

The doors to the throne room burst open. A man rushed in carrying a child in his arms. Lorelei thought the little boy didn't look right.

King Humphrey stood. "What or why—"

"Sire! I am a poor woodcutter! My son is sick, and I have no money to pay a wisewoman to cure him. I have nowhere to turn, except to you."

"Oh dear," Lorelei said. She ran to the child. "Does your forehead pulse?"

The boy nodded.

"Oh dear. Does it hurt to—"

Nicholas interrupted. "If you were a princess here," he asked the crocodile princess, "what would you do?"

This is the test! Lorelei thought. Maybe the boy wasn't really sick. But he looked sick.

The crocodile princess said, "They should be forbidden to trouble you with their problems. This man and his son must be put to death. That will cure the boy." And she smiled her slow smile.

"What would you do, Princess Lorelei?" Nicholas asked.

What was she supposed to say? Did that horrible one give the right answer? But if you couldn't help people – if you had to *kill* them to make them leave you alone – then she, Lorelei, didn't want to be a princess.

But then she'd have to give Nicholas up.

Well, it didn't matter what the right answer was. Somebody was sick! "Oh dear. I used to get sick when I was a little – uh – princess. I still do sometimes." She turned to the queen. "Do you have any betony?" Lorelei was sure she was ruining everything, because the queen looked so upset. "I need the leaves of the chaste tree, too. If you don't have that, some bugloss will do. Where's the kitchen?"

Queen Hermione didn't know what to say. So

she rang for the Chief Royal Serving Maid.

"Princess Lorelei would be kind to our subjects, Father," Nicholas said, while they waited for the serving maid. "Whether or not she can feel a pea under twenty mattresses." He dropped to his knees so hard, he thought he had broken a kneecap. "Ouch!"

"Oh dear," Lorelei said. A pea? What was he talking about?

"My darling princess." Nicholas took Lorelei's hand. "Will you marry me?"

"Oh dear. Yes, I'll marry you. We'll need hot water. Does your stomach ache?" she asked the boy.

He nodded.

"Did you sleep or rest well last night, Princess Lorelei?" the king asked. He had to know, even though everything had got confused or mixed up.

"No," Lorelei said. "I couldn't get comfortable. So I slept on the floor."

"The pea!" said the queen.

"The pea or bean," said the king.

"Darling!" said the prince.

Epilogue

*L*orelei cured the woodcutter's son. King Humphrey and Queen Hermione gave their consent or permission to the marriage of Prince Nicholas and Princess Lorelei.

On their wedding day Nicholas wore a doublet embroidered with parsley, a shirt embroidered with tape measures, and hose embroidered with noodles. Lorelei's hood and veil were embroidered with tuna fish. Her bodice was embroidered with green peas, and her skirt and train were embroidered with tiny mattresses.

Think jewels are cool?

Think again!

When a fairy gives Rosella the gift of jewels that fall from her lips every time she speaks, her life looks rosy. Her horrible twin sister Myrtle gets bugs and snakes instead – yeuch! So how come Rosella's miserable and Myrtle's never been happier?

stories turned
on their heads!

By the same author

Ella Enchanted
Spinning Tales ②
Princess Sonora and the Long Sleep
Cinderellis and the Glass Hill

SPINNING TALES

the Fairy's Mistake

GAIL CARSON LEVINE

An imprint of HarperCollins*Publishers*

First published as *The Princess Tales: The Fairy's Mistake*
in the USA by HarperCollins Children's Books 1999
First published in Great Britain by Collins 2001

3 5 7 9 10 8 6 4

Collins is an imprint of HarperCollins*Publishers* Ltd,
77-85 Fulham Palace Road, Hammersmith, London W6 8JB

The HarperCollins website address is www.fireandwater.com

ISBN 0 00 710946 6

Printed and bound in England by
Clays Ltd, St Ives plc

1

Once upon a time, in the village of Snettering-on-Snoakes in the kingdom of Biddle, Rosella fetched water from the well for the four thousand and eighty-eighth time.

Rosella always fetched the water because her identical twin sister, Myrtle, always refused to go. And their mother, the widow Pickering, never made

Myrtle do anything. Instead, she made Rosella do everything.

At the well the fairy Ethelinda was having a drink. When she saw Rosella coming, she changed herself into an old lady. Then she made herself look thirsty.

"Would you like a drink, Grandmother?" Rosella said.

"That would be lovely, dearie."

Rosella lowered her wooden bucket into the well. When she lifted it out, she held the dipper so the old lady could drink.

Ethelinda slurped the water. "Thank you. Your kindness merits a reward. From now—"

"You don't have..." Rosella stopped. Something funny was happening in her mouth. Had she lost a tooth? There was something hard under her tongue. And something hard in her cheek. "Excuse me." Now there was something in

her other cheek. She spat delicately into her hand.

They weren't teeth. She was holding a diamond and two opals.

"There, dearie," Ethelinda smiled. "Isn't that nice?"

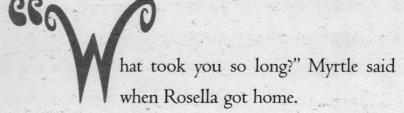

"W hat took you so long?" Myrtle said when Rosella got home.

"Your sister almost perished from thirst, you lazybones," their mother said.

"I gave a drink to..." Something was in Rosella's mouth again. It was between her lip and her front teeth this time. "I gave a drink to an old lady." An

emerald and another diamond fell out of her mouth. They landed on the dirt floor of the cottage.

"It was more important— What's that?" Myrtle said.

"What's that?" the widow said.

They both dived for the jewels, but Myrtle got there first.

"Rosella darling," the widow said, "sit down. Make yourself comfortable. Now tell us all about it. Don't leave anything out."

There wasn't much to tell, only enough to cover the bottom of Myrtle's teacup with gems.

"Which way did the old lady go?" Myrtle asked.

Rosella was puzzled. "She didn't go anywhere." An amethyst dropped into the teacup.

Myrtle grabbed the bucket and ran.

When she saw Myrtle in the distance, Ethelinda thought Rosella had come back. Only this time she wasn't tripping lightly down the path, smelling the

flowers and humming a tune. She was hurtling along, head down, arms swinging, bucket flying. And then Ethelinda's fairy powers told her that this was Rosella's twin sister. Ethelinda got ready by turning herself into a knight.

"Where did the old lady go?" Myrtle said when she reached the well.

"I haven't seen anyone. I've been alone, hoping some kind maiden would come by and give me a drink. I can't do it myself with all this armour."

"What's in it for me if I do?"

The fairy tilted her head. Her armour clanked. "The happiness of helping someone in need."

"Well, in that case, get your page to do it." Myrtle stomped off.

Ethelinda turned herself back into a fairy. "Your rudeness merits a punishment," she said. But Myrtle was too far away to hear.

Myrtle went through the whole village of

Snettering-on-Snoakes, searching for the old lady. The villagers knew she was Myrtle and not Rosella by her scowl and by the way she acted. Myrtle marched into shops and right into people's houses. She opened doors to rooms and even closets. Whenever anyone yelled at her, her only answer was to slam the door on her way out.

While Myrtle was in the village, Rosella went out to her garden to pick peas for dinner. As she worked, she sang.

> *Oh, May is the lovely month.*
> *Sing hey nonny May-o!*
> *Oh, June is the flower month.*
> *Sing hey nonny June-o!*
> *Oh, July is the hot month.*
> *Sing hey nonny July-o!*

And so on. While she sang, gems dropped from

her mouth. It still felt funny, but she was getting used to it. Except once she popped a pea into her mouth as she sang, and she almost broke a tooth on a ruby.

Rosella had a sweet voice, but Prince Harold, who happened to be riding by, wasn't musical. He wouldn't have stopped, except he spotted the sapphire trembling on Rosella's lip. He watched it tumble into the vegetables.

He tied his horse up at the widow Pickering's picket fence.

Rosella didn't see him, and she went on singing.

> *Oh, November is the harvest month.*
> *Sing hey nonny November-o!*
> *Oh, December is the last month,*
> *Sing hey…*

Prince Harold went into the garden. "Maiden…"
Rosella looked up from her peas. A man! A

nobleman! She blushed prettily.

She wasn't bad-looking, Prince Harold thought. "Pardon me," he said. "You've dropped some jewels. Allow me."

"Oh! Don't trouble yourself, Sir." Another sapphire and a moonstone fell out of Rosella's mouth.

Harold had a terrible thought. Maybe they were just glass. He picked up a stone. "May I examine this?"

Rosella nodded.

It didn't look like glass. It looked like a perfect diamond, five carats at least. But if the gems were real, why was she leaving them on the ground? He held up a jewel. "Maiden, is this really a diamond?"

"I don't know, Sir. It might be."

A topaz hit Prince Harold on the forehead. He caught it as it bounced off his chin. "Maiden, have jewels always come out of your mouth?"

Rosella laughed, a lovely tinkling sound. "Oh no, Sir. It only began this afternoon when an old lady — I think she may have been a fairy—"

They *were* real then! Harold knelt before her. "Maiden, I am Prince Harold. I love you madly. Will you marry me?"

3

osella didn't love the prince madly, but she liked him. He was so polite. And she thought it might be pleasanter to be a princess than to be the widow Pickering's daughter and Myrtle's sister. Besides, it could be against the law to say no to a prince. So she said yes, and dropped a garnet into his hand.

"I'm sorry, sweetheart. I didn't hear you."

"Yes, Your Highness."

Clink. Clink. Two more garnets joined Harold's collection. "You must say, 'Yes, Harold,' now that we're betrothed."

"Yes, Harold."

Clink.

The fairy Ethelinda was delighted that Rosella was going to be a princess. *She deserves it,* the fairy thought. Ethelinda was pleased with herself for having given Rosella the perfect reward.

The widow Pickering agreed to the marriage. But she insisted that Harold give her all the gems Rosella had produced before their engagement. The widow was careful not to mention Myrtle. She didn't want the prince to know that Rosella had a twin sister who would also have a jewel mine in her mouth. After all, what if he took Myrtle away too?

Prince Harold swung Rosella up on his horse. He

asked her to hold an open saddlebag on her lap. Then he mounted in front of her. As they rode off, he asked her about her garden, about the weather, about fly fishing, about anything.

The widow stood at the fence and waved her handkerchief. As she turned to go back into the cottage, she saw her favourite daughter in the distance. Myrtle was loping along, swinging the bucket. The widow opened the gate and followed her daughter into the house. "Darling, speak to me."

Myrtle sank into their only comfortable chair. "Hi, Mum. The stupid old lady wasn't—" There was a tickle in the back of her throat. What was going on? It felt like her tongue had got loose and was flopping around in her mouth. Could she be making jewels too? Did it happen just by going to the well? Whatever it was – diamond or pearl or emerald – it wanted to get out. Myrtle opened her mouth.

A garter snake slithered out.

The widow screamed and jumped on to their other chair. "Eeeeek! Get that thing out of here! Myrtle!" She pointed a shaking finger. "There it is! Get it! Eeeeek!"

Myrtle didn't budge. She stared at the snake coiling itself around a bedpost. How had this happened if the old lady wasn't at the well? The knight? The knight! The old lady had turned herself into a knight.

Myrtle jumped up and raced out, taking the bucket with her. "Bye, Mum," she called over her shoulder. "See you later." Two mosquitoes and a dragonfly flew out of her mouth.

The fairy Ethelinda watched Myrtle scurry down the road. She patted herself on the back for having given Myrtle the perfect punishment.

*P*rince Harold and Rosella reached the courtyard in front of the prince's palace. He lifted Rosella down from the horse.

"I'm too madly in love in wait," he said. "Let's announce our engagement first thing tomorrow morning, dear heart."

"All right," Rosella said.

Harold only got a measly seed pearl. "Princesses speak in complete sentences, darling."

Rosella took a deep breath for courage. "I'm tired. Your High— I mean Harold. May I rest for a day first?"

But Harold didn't listen. He was too interested in the green diamond in his hand. "I've never seen one of these before, honey bun. We can have the betrothal ceremony at nine o'clock sharp. Your Royal Ladies-in-Waiting will find you something to wear."

Harold snapped his fingers, and a Royal Lady-in-Waiting led Rosella away. They were on the castle doorstep when Harold ran after them.

"Angel, I almost forgot. What would you like served at our betrothal feast?"

Nobody had ever asked Rosella this kind of question before. She'd always had to eat scraps from her mother's and her sister's plates. Nobody had ever asked her what she liked to eat. Nobody had ever

asked her opinion about anything.

She smiled happily. "Your— I mean, Harold… uh… dear, I'd like poached quail eggs and roasted chestnuts for our betrothal feast." Six identical emeralds the colour of maple leaves in May dropped from Rosella's mouth.

The Royal Lady-in-Waiting, who was at Rosella's elbow, gasped.

"Look at these!" Harold said. "They're gorgeous. So you want wild boar for dinner?" He didn't give Rosella time to say she hated wild boar. "What do you know. It's my favourite too. I'll go tell the cook." He rushed off.

Rosella sighed.

The fairy Ethelinda, who was keeping an eye on things, sighed too.

Myrtle returned to the well, determined to give a drink to anybody who was there. But nobody was.

She lowered the bucket into the well anyway.

Nobody showed up.

She had an idea. It was worth a try. She watered the plants that grew around the well. "Dear plants," she began. "You look thirsty. Perhaps a little water would please you. It's no trouble. I don't mind, dear sweet plants."

Whatever was in her mouth was too big to be a jewel, unless it was the biggest one in the world. And a jewel wouldn't feel slimy on her tongue. She opened her mouth. A water bug crawled out. She closed her mouth, but there was more. More slime. She opened her mouth again. Two more water bugs padded out, followed by a black snake.

Giving the plants a drink hadn't done any good. Myrtle dumped the rest of the water on a rosebush. "Drown, you stupid plant," she muttered. A grasshopper landed on a rose.

Myrtle filled her bucket one more time. Then —

without saying a single word — she scoured the village again for the rotten fairy who'd done this to her. She swore to herself that she'd pour water down the throat of any stranger she found.

But there were no strangers, so Myrtle threw the bucket into the well and headed for home.

The widow was in the garden. She had dug up the peas and the radishes and the tomato plants. Now she was pawing through the roots, hoping to find some jewels that Prince Harold had missed. When she heard the gate slam shut, she stood up. "Don't say a word if you didn't find that old lady."

Myrtle closed her mouth with a snap. She picked up a stick and scratched in the dirt. "Where's Rosella?"

"She rode off to marry a prince. And like a fool, I let her go, because I thought I had you. You bungler, you idiot, you..."

That made Myrtle furious. How could she have

known the fairy would turn herself into a knight in so much armour you couldn't even see her – his – face? And hadn't she searched the village twice? And hadn't she watered those useless plants? Myrtle opened her mouth to give her mother what-for.

But the widow held up her hands and jumped back three feet. "Hush! Shh! Hush, my love. Perhaps I was hasty. We've both had a bad…"

Her mother's pleas gave Myrtle a new idea. She picked up the stick again and wrote, "Things are looking up, Mum. It will all be better tomorrow." She dropped the stick and started whistling – and wondering if whistling made snakes and insects too.

It didn't. Too bad, she thought.

Rosella was used to sleeping on the floor, because Myrtle and the widow had always taken the bed. In the palace she got her own bed. It had a canopy and three mattresses piled on top of each other and satin sheets and ermine blankets and pillows filled with swans' feathers.

So she should have got a fine night's sleep — except

that three Royal Guards stood at attention around her bed all night. One stood at each side of the bed, and one stood at the foot. If she talked in her sleep, they were supposed to catch the jewels and keep them safe for Prince Harold.

Rosella didn't talk in her sleep because she couldn't sleep with people watching her. By morning her throat felt scratchy. She thought she might be coming down with a cold.

Her twelve Royal Ladies-in-Waiting brought breakfast to her at seven o'clock. Scrambled eggs and wild-boar sausages. They shared the sausages while she ate the eggs. Rosella said "please" six times and "thank you" eight times. Each Royal Lady-in-Waiting got one jewel, and they fought over the remaining two.

"Nobody deserves that but me!" yelled one Royal Lady-in-Waiting.

"I work harder than any of you!" yelled another.

"I'm worth ten of each of you, so I should get everything!" shouted a third.

"You have some nerve, thinking…"

Rosella put her hands over her ears. She wished she could have ten minutes to herself.

Prince Harold came in. He coughed to get the attention of the Royal Ladies-in-Waiting. Nobody noticed except Rosella, who smiled at him. He'd be handsome, she thought, if he weren't so greedy.

The Royal Ladies-in-Waiting went on arguing.

"How dare you—"

"What do you mean—"

"The first person who—"

"SHUT UP!" Harold roared.

They did.

"You mustn't upset my bride." He went to Rosella, who was eating her breakfast in bed. He put his arm around her shoulder. "Are you all right, sugar plum?"

Rosella nodded. She liked the pet names he called her.

But she hoped he wouldn't make her say anything.

"Tell me so I'm sure, lovey-dove."

The fairy Ethelinda was worried.

Myrtle, on the other hand, had a great night's sleep. When she woke up, she put paper, a quill pen, and a bottle of ink in a pouch. Then she set out for the village. She'd have a fine breakfast when she got there, and she wouldn't pay a penny for it. As for the bucket she'd thrown down the well, why, she'd have her choice of buckets.

Her first stop was the baker's shop. She's scowling, the baker thought, so it's Myrtle. He scowled right back.

"Give me three of your freshest muffins," Myrtle said.

She has some nerve, the baker thought. Bossing me—What was coming out of her mouth? Ants! He grabbed his broom and swept them out of his store.

He tried to sweep Myrtle out too.

"Cut that out!" Myrtle said. A horsefly flew out of her mouth. A bedbug climbed over the edge of her lip and started down her chin.

The baker swatted the fly. He kept an eye on the bedbug, so he could kill it as soon as it touched the floor.

Myrtle took the pen and paper out of her pouch. "Give me the muffins and I won't say another word," she wrote. "I also want a fourteen-layer cake. It's for my party tomorrow, to celebrate my fourteen-year-and-six-weeks birthday. You're invited. Bring the whole family."

The baker swallowed hard and nodded. "I'll come. We'll all come. We'll be, uh, overjoyed to come." He wrapped up his most delicious muffins. When he handed them to Myrtle, he bowed.

The fairy Ethelinda was getting anxious. Punishments weren't supposed to work this way.

Rosella tried not to talk while she got ready for her betrothal, but her Royal Ladies-in-Waiting ignored her if she just pointed at things. They didn't yell at each other any more, because they didn't want Prince Harold to hear, but that didn't stop them from fighting quietly.

When Rosella said, "I'll wear that gown," two amazon stones and an opal fell to the carpet. And the twelve Royal Ladies-in-Waiting went for the jewels, hitting and shoving each other.

So Rosella took the gown out of the closet herself and laid it out on her bed. Then she stood over it, marvelling. It was silk, with an embroidered bodice. Its gathered sleeves ended in lace that would tickle her fingers delightfully. And the train was lace over silk, yards and yards of it.

"It's so pretty," she whispered. "It belongs in the sky with the moon and the stars."

Two pearls and a starstone fell into the deep folds of the gown's skirt. They were seen by a Royal Lady-in-Waiting who had taken a break from the fight on the carpet. She pounced on the gown.

The other Royal Ladies-in-Waiting heard the silk rustle. They pounced too. In less time than it takes to sew on a button, the gown lay in tatters on the bed.

Rosella wanted to scream, but she was afraid to. Screaming might make bigger and better gems. Then she'd have to scream all the time. Besides, her throat was really starting to hurt. She cried instead.

The fairy Ethelinda was getting angry. Rewards weren't supposed to work this way.

6

Rosella didn't mean to, but she dropped jewels on every gown in her princess wardrobe except one. And her Royal Ladies-in-Waiting ruined each of them. The one that was left was made of burlap and it was a size and a half too big. It didn't have a real train, but it did trail on the floor, because it was four inches too long.

Harold met Rosella in the palace's great hall, where the Chief Royal Councillor was going to perform the betrothal ceremony. The prince thought she looked pretty, with her brown wavy hair and her big grey eyes. But why had she picked the ugliest gown in the kingdom? It was big enough for her and a gorilla. All he said, though, was, "You look beautiful, honey bunch. Are you glad to be engaged?"

Rosella didn't know how to answer. Being engaged wasn't the problem, although marrying Harold might have its drawbacks. The problem was the jewels.

"Did you hear me, hon? I asked you a question." He raised his voice. "Are you happy, sweetheart?" He cupped his hand under her chin.

Rosella spoke through her teeth so the jewels wouldn't get out. "Everybody wants me to talk, but nobody listens to what I say."

"I'm listening, angel. Spit it out."

"I hate wild boar, and I don't want guards to stand around..." There were so many jewels in her mouth that one popped out, a hyacinth.

Harold put it in his pocket. The orchestra started to play.

She couldn't keep all these stones in her mouth. She spat them into her hand and made a fist.

"We're supposed to hold hands," Harold whispered. "Give them to me. I'll take good care of them."

What difference did it make? She let him have them.

The ceremony began.

Myrtle sat on the edge of the well to eat her muffins. After she ate them and licked her fingers, she headed for the stationer's shop. When she got there, an earwig and a spider bought her enough party invitations for everyone in the village. At the bottom

of each invitation she wrote, "Bring presents."

She gave out all the invitations and everyone promised to come. Then she stopped at the tailor's shop, where she picked out a gown for the party. It was white silk with an embroidered bodice and a lace train.

She was in such a good mood, she even bought a gown for her mother.

The fairy Ethelinda was furious.

At the end of the betrothal ceremony, the First Chancellor placed a golden tiara on Rosella's head. She wondered if she was a princess yet, or still just a princess-to-be.

"Some people want to meet you, honey," Harold said.

After a Royal Engagement, the kingdom's loyal subjects were always allowed into the palace to meet their future princess.

The Royal Guards opened the huge wooden doors to the great hall. Rosella saw a line that stretched for three quarters of a mile outside the palace. Everyone in it had something to catch the jewels as they cascaded out of her mouth. Pessimists brought thimbles and egg cups. Optimists brought sacks and pillowcases and lobster pots.

The first subject Rosella met was a farmer. "How are you?" he said.

"Fine." A ruby chip fell into his pail.

That was all? His shoulders slumped.

Rosella took pity on him. She said, "Actually my throat hurts, and this crown is giving me a headache."

He grinned as stones clattered against the bottom of his pail. Rosella asked him what he planned to do with the jewels.

"My old plough is worn out," he said. "I need a new one."

"Do you have enough now?" she said.

"Oh yes, Your Princess-ship. Thank you." He bowed and shook her hand.

Next in line was a woman whose skirt and blouse were as ragged as Rosella's had been yesterday. The woman wanted to buy a warm coat for the winter. Something about her made Rosella want to give her diamonds.

Rosella said, "Make sure your new coat is lined with fur. I think beaver is best." Diamond, she thought. Diamond, diamond.

But only one diamond came out, along with a topaz, some aquamarine stones, and some garnets. Thinking the name of the jewel didn't seem to make much difference. Anyway, the woman caught the stones in a threadbare sack and left happy.

A shoemaker came next, carrying a boot to catch the jewels. "What's your favourite flower?" he asked.

"Lilacs and carnations and daffodils," Rosella sang, wondering if singing would affect what came

out — a diamond, a ruby, and a turquoise on the large side.

The shoemaker said he had been too poor to buy leather to make any more shoes. "But now," he said, "I can buy enough to fill my shop window."

Rosella smiled. "And peonies and poppies and black-eyed Susans and marigolds and—"

She was starting to get the hang of it. Long vowels usually made precious jewels, while short vowels often made semiprecious stones. The softer she spoke, the smaller the jewels, and the louder the bigger. It really was a good thing she hadn't screamed at her Royal Ladies-in-Waiting.

"That's enough. Don't use them all up on me."

Rosella wished Harold would listen to this shoemaker. He could learn something.

Even though her throat hurt, she enjoyed talking to everybody. She liked her subjects! But why were so many of them poor?

Next was a boy who asked her to tell him a story. She made up a fable about a talkative parrot who lived with a deaf mouse. The boy listened and laughed in all the right places, and caught the jewels in his cap.

She smiled bravely and said hello to the next subject. Her throat hurt terribly.

he widow Pickering loved her new gown. She tried it on while Myrtle tried on her own new gown. The widow told Myrtle that she looked fantastic. Myrtle wrote that the new gown made her mother look twenty years younger.

They took off the gowns and hung them up so they wouldn't wrinkle. Then Myrtle went out into the

yard to experiment. She hummed softly. A line of ants pushed between her lips. She hummed louder, and the ants got bigger. Even louder, and the ants got even bigger. She'd had no idea there were such big ants. These were as big as her big toe.

Enough ants. Myrtle opened her mouth wide and sang, "La, la, la, la. Tra lee tra la tra loo." Moths, fireflies, and ladybugs flew out.

She hummed again. This time worms and caterpillars wriggled out. Hmmm. So she didn't always get ants by humming.

She tried speaking. "Nasty. Mean. Smelly. Rotten. Stupid. Loathsome." She giggled. "Vile. Putrid. Scabby. Mangy…"

They were crowding out – crawling, flitting, slithering, darting, wriggling, whizzing, oozing, flying, marching – escaping from Myrtle's mouth every way they could.

There were aphids, butterflies, mambas, lacewings,

lynx spiders, midges, wolf snakes, gnats, mayflies, rhinoceros vipers, audacious jumping spiders, bandy-bandy snakes, wasps, locusts, fleas, thrips, ticks, and every other bug and spider and snake you could think of.

Myrtle kept experimenting. She had a wonderful time, but she didn't figure out how to make a particular snake or insect come out. All she learned was that the louder she got, the bigger the creature that came out.

After about an hour, she had worked up quite an appetite. So she and her mother went to the village to have dinner at the inn. Dinner was free, because the innkeeper wanted to keep Myrtle from saying one single solitary word.

The fairy Ethelinda was scandalised.

During the betrothal banquet Harold noticed that Rosella's voice was fading. He noticed because all he

got were tiny gems, hardly more than shavings. So he didn't make her say much. But he did make her drink wild-boar broth.

"It's the best thing for you, tootsie," he said when she made a face.

She gulped it down and hoped it would stay there. She picked at her string beans. "Why are your subjects so poor?" she whispered. A tiny sapphire and bits of amber fell on to the tablecloth.

Harold brushed the jewels into his hand. His betrothed was sweet, but she didn't know much. Subjects were always poor. "I wish they were richer too, cutie pie. Then I could tax them more."

"Maybe we can help them." A pearl fell into Rosella's mashed potatoes.

Harold dug it out with his fork and rinsed it off in his mulled wine. "Honey, you'll wear yourself out worrying about them. Take it easy. Relax a little."

She fell asleep over dessert. Royal Servants carried

her to her bedchamber. But she woke up when the three Royal Guards took their places around her bed. Then she couldn't fall back to sleep.

8

Myrtle and the widow Pickering slept late the next morning. When they woke up, they strolled to the village. They stopped at the toymaker's shop for favours for the party guests. From the potter they ordered serving platters. The butcher promised them sausages and meat pies. By noon they had picked out everything for the party.

Then they linked arms and sauntered home.

The fairy Ethelinda gnashed her teeth.

By morning Rosella's throat hurt worse than ever. She thought she had a fever, too. But her voice was stronger.

Breakfast was wild-boar steak and eggs. Before her Royal Ladies-in-Waiting had taken ten bites, Harold sent for her.

He was waiting in the library. As soon as she went in, she became very scared. There were thousands of books, but they weren't what scared her. She liked books. There were four desks. That was fine, too. There were a dozen upholstered leather chairs, and they looked comfortable enough. A Royal Manservant and a Royal Maid were dusting. They were all right.

The terrifying sight was the fifteen empty chests lined up in front of one of the leather chairs.

"Sweetie pie," Harold said. "Am I glad to see you."

He led her to the chair behind the empty chests. "Wait till I tell you my idea."

Rosella sat down.

"Did you have a good breakfast, cuddle bunch?"

It hurt too much to talk. She shook her head.

Harold was too excited to pay attention. "Good. Here's my idea. You've noticed how old and mouldy this palace is?"

She shook her head.

"You haven't? Well, it is. The drawbridge creaks. The rooms are draughty. The cellars are full of rats. The place should be condemned."

She didn't say anything. The palace looked fine to her.

"So I had a brainstorm. You didn't know you were marrying a genius, did you?"

She shook her head.

"This is brilliant. Listen. We're going to build a new castle. That's my idea. Picture it. Cream-coloured

stone. Marble everywhere. Hundreds of fountains. Taller towers than anybody ever heard of. Crocodiles and serpents in the moat. People will travel thousands of miles to see it. You'll be famous, sweetheart."

"Me?"

Harold caught the tiny ruby. "Yes, you. I can't build a palace on current revenues. We need your voice. The kingdom needs you. So just make sure they land in the chests, will you, sugar?"

She was silent.

"I know. You're wondering how you'll ever think of things to say to fill fifteen chests. That's why we're in the library. All you have to do is read out loud. Here." He pulled a book off the shelf. "This looks interesting. *The History of the Monarchy in the Kingdom of Biddle.* That's us, love." He put the book in her lap. "You can read about our family."

She didn't open it. What could he do to her if she didn't talk? He could throw her in a dungeon. She

wouldn't mind if he did. Bread and water would be better than wild boar. Then again, he could chop off her head, which would hurt her throat even more than it was hurting now.

"I know you're tired, darling. But after you fill these chests, you can take a vacation. You won't have to say a word." He got down on one knee. "Please, sweetheart. Pretty please."

He has his heart set on a new palace, Rosella thought. He'll be miserable if he doesn't get one, and it will be because of me. Rosella opened the book to the middle. I'm too kindhearted, she thought. She started reading, trying to speak around her sore throat. "The fourth son of King Beauregard the Hairy weighed seven pounds and eleven ounces at birth. He had a noodle-shaped birthmark on his left shoulder. He waited for…"

A stream of jewels fell into the chest. Harold tiptoed out of the room.

Rosella went on reading. "The infant was named Durward. His first word, 'More,' proved him to be..." She was freezing. She looked up. The fire looked hot. "...proved him to be a true royal son. His tutors reported..." The room was spinning. "...reported that he excelled at archery, hunting..." What was wrong with this book? The letters were getting bigger and smaller. The lines of print were wavy. "...hunting, and milit—"

Rosella fainted and fell off her chair.

The Royal Manservant and Royal Maid rushed to the partly filled chest. They each grabbed a handful of jewels. Then the Royal Manservant ran to find Harold, while the Royal Maid used her apron to fan Rosella.

"Wake up, Your Highness. Please wake up," she cried.

9

The fairy Ethelinda was appalled. This was the last straw. She had to do something.

Harold was in the courtyard, practising his swordplay. She materialised in front of him. She didn't bother to disguise herself, hoping he'd be terrified when he saw the works — all seven feet three inches of her, her fleshy pink wings, the shimmer in

the air around her, the purple light she was always bathed in, her flashing wand.

"You're a fairy, right?" Harold said when he saw her. He didn't seem frightened.

"I am the fairy Ethelinda," she said, lowering her voice to a roar.

Harold grinned. "Pretty good guessing on my part, considering I've never met a fairy before."

"I am the one who made the jewels come out of Rosella's mouth."

Harold almost jumped up and down, he was so excited. "That was you? Really? Uh, say, Ethel... tell me, what did my sweetie pie do to make you do it?"

"My name is *Ethelinda*," the fairy boomed. "I rewarded her after she gave me a drink of well water."

"I can do that. That's a—"

"I'm not thirsty. Do you know that you're making poor Rosella miserable?"

"She's not miserable. She's a princess. She's deliriously happy."

Ethelinda tried a different approach. "Why do you want jewels so much?"

"You wouldn't want them?"

"Not if it was making my betrothed unhappy."

"How could she be unhappy? If I were in her shoes, I'd be delighted. She wouldn't be a princess today if I hadn't come along. She gets to wear a crown. She has nice gowns, Royal Ladies-in-Waiting. And me."

"You have to stop making her talk."

"But she has to talk. That's what makes *me* happy."

Ethelinda raised her wand. Prince Harold was one second away from becoming a frog. Then she lowered it. Her self-confidence was gone. If she turned him into a frog, he might figure out a way to make it better than being a prince. She certainly

didn't want to reward him the way she'd rewarded Myrtle.

She didn't know what to do.

The Royal Manservant who'd seen Rosella faint finally reached the courtyard. He ran to Harold.

Ethelinda vanished.

Myrtle's party started at two o'clock. The schoolteacher arrived first. His present was a slate and ten boxes of coloured chalk.

Myrtle opened one of the boxes. She wrote on the slate in green and orange letters, "Thank you. I'll let you know when I run out of chalk."

The baker came next. His cake was so big that it barely fitted through the cottage doorway. The icing was chocolate. The decorations were pink and blue whipped cream. The writing on top said, "Happy Fourteen-and-Six-Weeks Birthday, Myrtle! Please Keep Quiet!"

The whole village came. Nobody wanted to take a chance on making Myrtle mad. The guests filled the cottage and the yard and the yards of the surrounding cottages. The widow thanked them all for coming. Myrtle collected her presents. She smiled when anyone handed her an especially big box.

The food was the finest anybody could remember. Myrtle ate so many poached quail eggs and roasted chestnuts that she almost got sick. After everybody ate, she opened her presents. There were hundreds of them. Her favourites were:

The framed sampler that read, "Speak to me only with thine eyes."

The bouquet of mums.

The music box that played "Hush Little Baby."

The silver quill pen, engraved with the motto "The pen is mightier than the voice."

The parrot that sat on Myrtle's shoulder and

repeated over and over, "Shut your trap. Shut your trap. Shut your trap."

The charm bracelet with the golden letters S, I, L, E, N, C, and E.

After all the presents were opened, everybody sang "Happy Birthday". Myrtle was so thrilled that she smiled and clapped her hands.

Rosella was gravely ill, and Harold was seriously frightened. Even under mounds of swansdown quilts, she couldn't stop shivering. She felt as if a vulture's claws were scratching at her throat and a carpenter hammering at her temples.

The Royal Physician was called in to examine her. When he was finished, he told Harold that she was very sick. He said her only hope of recovery lay in bed rest and complete silence. His fee for the visit was the jewels he collected when he listened to her chest and made her say "Aah" sixteen times.

Myrtle had a birthday party every week. She and the widow laughed and laughed at their silliness in wishing for jewels to come out of Myrtle's mouth. When Myrtle got bored between parties, she would speak into a big jar. Then she'd let the bugs and the snakes loose in the yard and make them race. She and her mother would have a grand time

betting on the winners.

Rosella got better so slowly that Ethelinda's patience snapped. The evening after Myrtle's fourth party, Ethelinda materialised as herself in the widow's cottage. "I am the fairy Ethelinda, who rewarded your sister and punished you. You have to help Rosella," she thundered.

Myrtle sneered. "I do? I have to?"

A bull snake slithered under Ethelinda's gown. A gnat bit her wing.

"Ouch!" Ethelinda yelped.

"Be careful, dear," the widow told Myrtle. "You might make a poisonous snake."

"Yes, you have to help her," Ethelinda said. "Or I'll punish you severely."

Myrtle wrote on her slate, "I like your punishments."

"I can take your punishment away," Ethelinda said.

As fast as she could, Myrtle wrote, "What do I have to do?"

Ethelinda explained the problem.

"I can fix that," Myrtle wrote.

Ethelinda transported Myrtle to the palace, where Rosella was staring up at her lace bed canopy and wondering when her night-time guards would arrive. As Ethelinda and Myrtle materialised, Ethelinda turned herself back into the old lady.

"I've brought your sister to help you, my dear," Ethelinda said.

Rosella stared at them. Myrtle would never help her.

Myrtle had brought her slate with her. She wrote, "Change clothes with me and hide under the covers."

Rosella didn't move. She wondered if she was delirious.

"Go ahead. Do it," Ethelinda said. "She won't hurt you."

Rosella nodded. She put on Myrtle's silk nightdress with the gold embroidery and slipped deep under the blankets. Myrtle got into Rosella's silk nightdress with the silver embroidery.

Myrtle climbed into Rosella's bed. She sat up and yodelled, long and loud. A hognose snake wriggled out of her mouth.

Harold heard her, even though he was at the other end of the palace. He started running, leaping, and skipping toward the sound. "She's better! She's well again!" he yelled. And how many jewels did that yodel make? he wondered.

Ethelinda made the snake disappear. Then she made herself invisible.

"Precious!" Harold said, coming through the door. He dashed to the bed. "The roses are back in your cheeks. Speak to me!"

"What roses?" Myrtle yelled as loud as she could. "I feel terrible." The head of a boa constrictor

filled her mouth.

Harold jumped back. "Aaaa! What's that?"

Rosella lifted a tiny corner of blanket so she could watch. The snake slithered out and wound itself around Myrtle's waist.

Myrtle grinned at Harold. "Do you like him? Should I name him after you?" Three hornets flew straight at him. One of them stung him on the nose. The other two buzzed around his head.

"Ouch! Wh-what's going on... h-honey pie? Th-that's a s-snake. Wh-where did the j-jewels go? Why are b-bugs and snakes coming out?"

This is fun, Myrtle thought. Who'd have thought I could scare a prince?

Poor Harold, Rosella thought. But it serves him right. He looks so silly. She fought back a giggle and wished she could make a bug come out of her mouth once in a while.

"I'm angry. This is what happens when I get

angry." A scorpion stuck its head out of Myrtle's mouth.

"Yow! Why are you angry? At me? What did I do?"

"It's not so great being a princess," Myrtle yelled. "Nobody listens to me. All they care about are the jewels. You're the worst. It's all you care about, too. And I don't want to eat wild boar ever again. I hate wild boar."

The air was so thick with insects that Harold could hardly see. Snakes wriggled across the carpets. Snakes slithered up the sconces. Snakes oozed down the tapestries. A gigantic one hung from the chandelier, its head swaying slowly.

A milk snake slipped under the covers. It settled its clammy body next to Rosella. She wanted to scream and run. Instead, she bit her lip and stayed very, very still.

"Sweetheart, I'm sorry. Forgive me. Ouch! That hurt."

Myrtle screamed, "I'M NOT GOING TO TALK UNLESS I WANT TO!"

"All right. All right! You won't have to. And I'll listen to you. I promise." Something bit his foot all the way through his boot. He hopped and kicked to get rid of it. "Everyone will listen. By order of Prince Harold."

"AND PRINCESS ROSELLA," Myrtle yelled.

"And Princess Rosella," Harold echoed.

Myrtle lowered her voice. "Now leave me. I need my rest."

11

After Harold left, Ethelinda made the snakes and bugs disappear. Rosella came out from under the covers.

"Thank you," Rosella told her sister. An emerald fell on the counterpane.

Myrtle snatched the jewel and said, "You're welcome." She snagged the fly before it got to

Rosella's face. Then she crushed it in her fist.

"You've done a good deed," Ethelinda began.

Myrtle shook her head. "Don't reward me. Thanks, but no thanks." She let two cockroaches fall into the bed.

Ethelinda asked if Myrtle would help Rosella again if she needed it.

"Why should I?" Myrtle asked.

"I'll pay you," Rosella said.

Myrtle pocketed the two diamonds. Not bad. She'd get to frighten the prince again and get jewels for it, too. "OK."

Myrtle and Rosella switched clothes again. Then Ethelinda sent Myrtle back home. When Myrtle was gone, Ethelinda said she had to leave too. She vanished.

Rosella sank back into her pillows. She didn't want Myrtle to help again, or even Ethelinda. She wanted to solve the problem of Harold and his poor subjects all by herself.

Harold didn't dare visit Rosella again that day. But he did command the Royal Servants to listen to her. So Rosella got rid of her night-time guards. And she had her meal of poached quail eggs and roasted chestnuts at last.

She also ordered the Royal Ladies-in-Waiting to bring her a slate and chalk. From then on, she wrote instead of talking to them. She was tired of having them dive into her lap whenever she said anything.

And she had them bring her a box with a lock and key. She kept the box and the slate by her side so she'd be ready when Harold came.

He showed up a week after Myrtle's visit. Rosella felt fine by then. She was sitting at her window, watching a juggler in the courtyard.

"Honey?" He poked his head in. He was ready to run if the room was full of creepy-crawlies. But the coast seemed clear, so he stepped in all the way. He was carrying a bouquet of daisies and a box of taffy. "All

better, sweetheart?" He held the daisies in front of his face — in case any hornets started flying.

He looks so scared, Rosella thought. She smiled to make him stop worrying.

He lowered the bouquet cautiously and placed it on a table. Then he sat next to her and looked her over. She seemed healthy. That silk nightdress was cute. Blue was a good colour for her.

He hoped she wasn't feeling miserable any more. Anyone who was going to marry him should be the happiest maiden in the kingdom. He still wanted her to talk up enough jewels for a new palace. Then, after that, he wouldn't mind a golden coach and a few other items. But he wanted her to be happy, too.

They sat there, not saying anything.

"Oh, here," Harold said finally. He held out the bouquet and the sweets.

She took them. "Thank you."

An opal hovered on her lip and tumbled out. Harold

reached for it, but Rosella was faster. She opened her box and dropped in the opal. It clinked against the stones already in there. She snapped the box shut.

That was pretty selfish of her, Harold thought. He started to get mad, but then he thought of boa constrictors and hornets. He calmed down. "What's the box for, darling?"

"My jewels." A pearl came out this time. A big one. It went into the box too.

"Honey… Sweetie pie… What are you going to do with them?"

"Give them away. Your subjects need them more than we do."

"NO YOU DON'T!" Harold hollered. She couldn't! It was all right to give jewels away for the engagement ceremony. That was once in a lifetime, but she wanted to make a habit of it. "You can't give them away. I won't allow it."

Rosella wrote on her slate, "I'm trying not to get angry."

"No, no, don't get mad!" Harold started backing away. "But don't you want a new palace? I'll tell you what — we'll name a wing after you. It'll be the Rosella Wing. How do you like that?"

She shook her head. "This palace is beautiful. Look at it! It's wonderful."

All those gems going into the box! thought Harold. Wasted! If she gave them away, soon his subjects would be richer than he was. "Tell you what," Harold said. "We'll split fifty-fifty."

"I won't read a million books out loud just to fill up your treasure chests."

He counted as they fell. Two diamonds, three bloodstones, one hyacinth, and one turquoise.

He sighed. "All right, my love."

"All right, my love. Fifty-fifty." Rosella wanted to be fair. He had made her a princess, after all.

They shook hands. Then they kissed.

Epilogue

yrtle never had to come to her sister's rescue ever again. The fifty-fifty deal worked out perfectly. Harold got his new palace and golden coach, eventually. And Rosella was happy talking to her subjects and making sure they had enough ploughs and winter coats and leather for making shoes. Also, she built them a new school and a library and a swimming pool.

In time she and Harold grew to love each other very much. Harold even stopped trying to steal the

jewels from Rosella's wooden box while she was sleeping. And Rosella stopped counting them every morning when she woke up.

Myrtle and her mother went into the bug-and-snake-racing business. People came from twenty kingdoms to watch Myrtle's races. They'd bet beetles against spiders or rattlers against pythons or grasshoppers against garter snakes. The widow would call the races, and Myrtle would take the bets. The whole village got rich from the tourist trade. And Myrtle became truly popular, which annoyed her.

Ethelinda grew more careful. Myrtle was her last mistake. Nowadays when she punishes people, they stay punished. And when she rewards them, they don't get sick.

And they all lived happily ever after.

The End

Trudy (who was perfectly safe, of course) was furious that she hadn't got rid of Lorelei. But when she moved into the castle, the other Royal Servants showed her the good side of serving a bunch of persnickety monarchs. She learned to agree with them over a dinner of cream of asparagus soup, venison crown roast, and twelve-layer mocha-raspberry cake.

When Sam returned from the earldom of Pildenue, he moved into the palace too. He never understood exactly how Lorelei had become a princess. And he couldn't for the life of him understand why everyone called him Lord Blacksmith. But he liked living in a palace and shoeing the king's wonderful horses.

So they all lived happily ever after.

The End